OH BEANS!
St★rring Jelly Bean

BY ELLEN WEISS • ILLUSTRATED BY SUSAN T. HALL

Troll Associates

Jelly Bean just loved to play jokes on his friends. He wasn't a mean bean. He just thought it was very, very funny to give someone an awful surprise.

Every day of the week, you could count on Jelly Bean to play a practical joke.

On Monday, he ripped a piece of paper while Boston Bean was bending over.

Jelly Bean thought it was really a scream.

Boston Bean thought his pants had ripped open.

On Tuesday, he switched the sugar and salt on Half-Baked Bean's breakfast table.

Jelly Bean thought, "What a funny idea!"

Half-Baked Bean thought his grapefruit tasted awful.

On Wednesday, he hid behind the bushes in front of Vanilla Bean's house. When Vanilla Bean got home from a Bruce Springbean concert, Jelly Bean jumped up and scared her.

Jelly Bean thought it was his best joke ever.

Vanilla Bean thought a horrible monster had come to get her.

On Thursday, Jelly Bean balanced a bucket of water over String Bean's door. When String Bean got home from the Beanum and Bailey Circus, she got a brand-new hairdo.

On Friday, Jelly Bean hid all Snap Bean's underwear.

On Saturday, it was Jelly Bean's birthday.

"Oh boy, oh joy!" thought Jelly Bean. "I wonder what my friends have planned."

Jelly Bean thought about all the presents he was going to get for his birthday. "Maybe I'll get that new beanie, or a soft, cuddly teddy bean."

Jelly Bean tidied up his house for the friends who'd be coming to visit.

There was a knock at the door. "Are you home, Jelly Bean?" called Vanilla Bean. "I came to borrow a cup of sugar."

"A cup of sugar!" thought Jelly Bean excitedly. "She must be baking me a birthday cake!"

"I'm baking a cake for Uncle Beanjamin," Vanilla Bean explained. "Thanks for helping me out."

Jelly Bean poured himself a big bowl of Beanios for breakfast. "No sense saving room for my birthday cake," he said to himself. "I never thought Vanilla Bean would forget my birthday."

"Maybe I'll zip over to the mailbox," he thought. "I'm sure there'll be some birthday cards for me."

But there were no cards. And no one in sight, except Half-Baked Bean, hurrying by.

"Oh, um, hi there, Jelly Bean," said Half-Baked Bean. "I was just going to—um—the grocery store."

"What a half-baked story," thought Jelly Bean. "He's walking in the wrong direction. He forgot my birthday too."

As Jelly Bean walked back to his house, he saw Snap Bean standing outside.

"Do you have any candles?" Snap Bean asked. "My light bulb has just burned out."

"Too bad," said Jelly Bean, as he gave him some candles, "this *bean* a special day and all."

"Nothing special about it!" snapped Snap Bean, and off he went with the candles.

As time ticked away, the shadows got longer in front of Jelly Bean's house.

The telephone rang. Jelly Bean popped up.

"Hello?" he said eagerly.

"Hi, Jelly," said String Bean. "Boston Bean and I need balloons for our science project. Do you have some we can borrow?"

"Sure," said Jelly Bean sadly.

Jelly Bean was miserable. His friends had forgotten his birthday! He was all washed up. He was nothing but a has-bean.

Silently and slowly, he took last Tuesday's bran muffin out of the refrigerator. It felt like a brick. He found the very last candle in the drawer and pounded it into the top of the muffin. Then he lit the candle.

"Happy Birthday to me," he sang in a mournful voice, "Happy Birthday to me, Happy Birthday to Jelly Bean, Happy Birthday to—"

DING DONG! DING DONG!

Jelly Bean's doorbell rang madly. Before he could even get out of his chair, the door burst wide open.

There stood his friends, holding piles and piles of presents, and a great big birthday cake. They watched Jelly Bean's eyes pop, and they laughed and laughed.

"Surprise!" they all yelled. "The joke's on you, Jelly Bean!"

"We never forgot your birthday," laughed Boston Bean.

"We just wanted to play a joke on you, the way you play jokes on us," said Snap Bean.

"But now it's time to eat cake and have fun!" said Vanilla Bean.

"Gee whiz," said Jelly Bean, his mouth stuffed with birthday cake. "You really out-tricked me. But I learned my lesson. Bean a joker isn't always funny—when you're on the other side."